THE MISSING
MONEY MYSTERY

NANCY DREW®/THE HARDY BOYS®

Be A Detective Mystery Stories™

#6

THE MISSING MONEY MYSTERY

by
Carolyn Keene and
Franklin W. Dixon

Illustrated by Paul Frame

WANDERER BOOKS
Published by Simon & Schuster, Inc., New York

Published by WANDERER BOOKS
A Division of Simon & Schuster, Inc.
Simon & Schuster Building
1230 Avenue of the Americas
New York, New York 10020

Designed by Stanley S. Drate

Manufactured in the United States of America

10 9 8 7 6 5 4 3 2

WANDERER and colophon are registered trademarks
of Simon & Schuster Inc.

NANCY DREW, NANCY DREW MYSTERY STORIES, and
THE HARDY BOYS are trademarks of Simon & Schuster, Inc.
registered in the United States Patent and Trademark Office.
BE A DETECTIVE MYSTERY STORIES is a trademark of
Simon & Schuster, Inc.

Library of Congress Cataloging in Publication Data

Keene, Carolyn.
    The missing money mystery.

    (Nancy Drew/the Hardy boys be a detective mystery
stories)
    Summary. A self-directing adventure starring Nancy
Drew and the Hardy brothers, who are investigating the
disappearance of a briefcase full of money.
    1. Plot-your-own stories.   [1. Plot-your-own stories.
2. Mystery and detective stories]   I. Dixon, Franklin W.
II. Frame, Paul.   III. Title.   IX. Series: Keene, Carolyn.
Nancy Drew/the Hardy boys be a detective mystery
stories ;
PZ7.K23Mi 1985   [Fic]   84-29111
ISBN 0-671-54551-5

Dear Fans,

Since so many of you have written to us saying how much you want to be detectives like Nancy Drew and The Hardy Boys, we figured out a way. Of course, we had to put our heads together to create mysteries that were so baffling they needed help from everyone including Nancy, Frank, Joe, and you!

In these exciting new BE A DETECTIVE MYSTERY STORIES, you'll be part of a great team of amateur sleuths following clues and wily suspects. At every turn, you'll have a chance to pick a different trail filled with adventure that may lead to danger, surprise, or an amazing discovery!

The choices are all yours—see how many there are and have fun!

C.K. and F.W.D.

"**A** briefcase full of hundred-dollar bills!" Nancy Drew exclaimed, her blue eyes wide with surprise.

"Yes. I saw the money," Jill Blake insisted. "But there's no way I can prove it."

The two girls were sitting on the patio of the Blakes' house along with their friends Frank and Joe Hardy.

"Tell us exactly what happened," dark-haired Frank suggested, sipping a glass of cold lemonade.

"Well, my neighbor, Lila Lewis, asked me to keep an eye on her house while she's in Europe," seventeen-year-old Jill began. "Last night, I walked over there to check on the place and let myself in with the key she had given me. That's when I saw the briefcase full of money on a table in the living room."

"What did you do?" Joe inquired.

"I went to ask Peter, the gardener, about it. I had seen him on the premises earlier and figured he was still around."

"Did you find him?" Nancy inquired.

"No. He had left. When I went back into the house, the briefcase was gone!"

Turn to page 2.

2

"Wow!" Joe exclaimed, and ran a hand through his blond hair. "All that money vanished into thin air!"

"Could we go over to the house?" Frank asked. "I'd like to see if there are any clues."

"Sure," Jill said. "You'll like the place. It's really beautiful. And in case you wonder about the heart-shaped swimming pool—Lila was a big movie star in the forties."

Nancy laughed. She and the Hardys had arrived at the Blakes' that morning. Jill and her father, who was on a business trip, lived in the hills above Los Angeles, and the three young detectives had decided to pay a visit to Jill before meeting Mr. Hardy in Santa Clara two days later. Now their day promised to turn out even more exciting than they had expected because of the strange goings-on next door!

Turn to page 3.

Jill went inside to get the key, then led the way to the adjoining property. As they approached the back door, Joe Hardy noticed a man pruning a hedge.

3

"Is that Peter, the gardener?" he asked Jill.

"Yes. He's been working for Miss Lewis for two years now," the girl replied.

Just then the man looked up. He was wearing a worried look on his face. Jill waved a greeting, then opened the door leading into the house.

The detectives followed her inside to the table where the suitcase had been. Frank and Joe began to search the area, while Jill turned to Nancy with a concerned look on her face.

"There's one other thing I should tell you," she began hesitantly. "I saw a man running from the house while I was looking for Peter."

Turn to page 4.

4

"Did you recognize him?" Nancy asked.

"I'm not sure . . . ," Jill murmured. "There was only moonlight to see by. But it could have been Lila's grandson, Jack Turner. He's in the movie business and has long, curly hair . . . just like the fleeing man had."

"Why didn't you mention this earlier?" the titian-blonde sleuth inquired curiously.

"I didn't want to accuse Jack," Jill replied. "He's always been very nice to me."

Just then, Joe bent down and picked up something from beneath the large, low table.

"Look at this, Frank," he exclaimed, showing a small, shiny object to his brother.

Turn to page 5.

"It's a silicon chip," Frank said, "for a computer. Why would that be here under the table?"

Joe shrugged. "I don't know. But it reminds me of the case Dad is coming to investigate here. It involves high-tech espionage."

5

"I think you and I should go to Silicon Valley," Frank suggested, referring to the Santa Clara Valley in California where most of the nation's computer firms were headquartered. "Perhaps we can learn who made the chip."

"I'd like to find out more about Jack Turner," Nancy spoke up. "There are several big movie lots outside of Los Angeles."

"We can't ignore the gardener, either," Joe reminded them. "He's a likely suspect, and he looked pretty worried when we saw him a few minutes ago."

"One way or another," Nancy assured Jill, "we'll find out what happened to that mysterious briefcase full of money!"

If you want to follow Nancy to the movie lots to investigate Jack Turner, turn to page 10.
If you want to follow Frank and Joe to Silicon Valley, turn to page 7.
If you think the sleuths should investigate the gardener, turn to page 6.

6

"Can you tell us anything else about Peter, the gardener?" Joe asked Jill.

"Well," the dark-haired girl replied, "he lives on the grounds in a little cottage attached to the garage."

"Is that where you tried to find him yesterday?" Nancy inquired.

"Yes, but as I told you, he had left," Jill answered.

"Let's ask him a few questions," Frank suggested. "I'd like to know what his alibi is for last night."

Turn to page 12.

"It just doesn't make sense," Frank said thoughtfully, "that this computer chip was here."

"I wish we could get a lead to work on before going all the way to Silicon Valley," Joe added. "It's a long drive."

"Does Jack Turner have anything to do with computers?" Nancy asked Jill.

"No, I don't think so," the dark-haired girl responded. "But I remember Miss Lewis mentioning a relative once . . . she said he was a real computer genius."

Frank's eyes lit up with curiosity.

"Do you remember who it was?" he questioned.

"No, I don't. But I'll call Dad when we go back to the house. He may recall the name."

"Great! Let's go," Joe said impatiently.

Turn to page 14.

8

"I'd like to see Barlow's office," Joe requested, "and investigate it for clues." Frank nodded in agreement.

"Follow me," Eric Barnes said, and led the boys down a series of corridors to the research section. On the way, the executive described the company's safety measures.

"There are several levels of security built into our main data bank," he explained. "Secret passwords are needed to gain access at each level. Unfortunately, Barlow has the key word necessary to obtain any kind of information he wants."

Several minutes later, the three arrived at a metal door with the words "No Admittance" on it. Eric Barnes pulled a plasic card out of his pocket and pushed it into the slot of a black computerized box. Orange letters reading "Clearance Approved" flashed on a screen, then the door automatically opened.

Joe cast an excited glance at his brother as they walked into Tri-Tech's research section. The room was filled with men and women intently working in front of computers. On the monitors were all sorts of amazing simulations and graphics.

Turn to page 9.

"Wow!" Joe exclaimed. "This place is right out of the future."

The two brothers gazed at several of the monitors with fascination, then had to hurry to catch up with Eric Barnes. He had walked into a glass-walled office on the far side of the room.

"Here's where Barlow works," the vice-president announced when the Hardys arrived. "Look around as much as you want. I have to get back to my office. I'm going to inform security to monitor the computer access codes. I want to know if Barlow tries to use the data bank."

The two detectives began to search the office for clues.

"Look at that picture," Frank said, pointing to a photo of a young man and woman on the beach. "I'll bet that's Craig Barlow . . . and check out the haircut!"

"He fits the description of the man Jill Blake saw fleeing from Lila Lewis's home last night," Joe added.

Turn to page 22.

10

"There's a lot of big money in the movie industry," Nancy murmured thoughtfully. "Jack Turner could be involved in some illegal payoff."

"He works at a studio just west of Los Angeles," Jill explained. "I can lend you my car if you want to drive there."

"Thanks," the girl detective replied. Then she glanced at several photographs sitting on a baby grand piano nearby.

"Is one of these pictures of Jack Turner?" she asked as she walked over to study them.

"Yes," Jill answered, pointing to a portrait of a young man.

Joe peered over Nancy's shoulder. "Jack looks like a rock star," he commented.

Jill giggled and said, "So do a lot of other people in Los Angeles!"

Nancy walked over to a telephone table and opened the directory. She quickly leafed through the book until she found the name she was looking for.

"Great!" she exclaimed. "Jack Turner's number and address are listed here. I'd like to drive by his place and check it for clues."

"Okay," Jill said. "Come back to my house and I'll give you my car keys."

Turn to page 11.

The three detectives followed her out of the Lewis mansion. As they walked back through the garden, Nancy thought about her plan of action.

11

"I'm not sure where I should go first," she said. "I might catch Jack Turner at home and surprise him, or I could go to the movie studio and investigate there."

If you think Nancy should drive to the movie studio, turn to page 23.
If you think she should investigate Jack Turner's house first, turn to page 37.

12

The three sleuths and Jill left the house and went to the place where the gardener had been working earlier. He was gone!

"Maybe he's in his cottage," Nancy said, noticing the small building to the right of the house.

Just then, they heard the sound of a car engine starting up. Frank, Joe, and Nancy sprinted to the garage, where Peter was backing away in a brown compact car.

"I have a hunch," Frank murmured, "that Joe and I should follow him. Hurry up, brother, let's get our car."

"I'll stay here," Nancy added, "and see what I can find in the cottage."

If you want to go with Frank and Joe, turn to page 16.
If you want to stay with Nancy, turn to page 21.

14

The three young detectives followed Jill Blake through the garden of the Lewis mansion. When they arrived at the Blake house, the young girl immediately phoned her father.

"Craig Barlow, now I remember," she said into the receiver. "Thanks a lot, Dad . . . yes, I'll be careful."

After Jill had hung up, she described her conversation to the others.

"Dad said Lila Lewis has a nephew named Craig Barlow. She's always been very proud of him because he's so intelligent."

"Did your father say where this Craig Barlow works?" Frank inquired.

"Yes," Jill replied. "He's employed by Tri-Tech Industries as a computer research engineer."

Excitement flashed across the Hardys' faces.

"I think we've got the lead we needed!" Joe exclaimed. "That's the company outside Santa Clara that Dad's working for!"

"Let's not waste any more time," Frank urged. "I want to drive up to Tri-Tech today before it closes!"

Turn to page 15.

Several hours later, Frank swung their white rental car into the Tri-Tech complex.

"Let's go straight to the office of Eric Barnes," Joe suggested. "He's the vice-president who contacted Dad."

The brothers parked their car and went through the glass door of the main building. The architecture of the complex was streamlined and contemporary, and the walls of the lobby were lined with photographs of computer graphics.

"We'd like to see Mr. Eric Barnes, please," Joe told the receptionist.

Minutes later, the boys were shown into a large office decorated with expensive white leather furniture.

"So you're Fenton Hardy's famous sons!" a dark-haired man in his forties declared as he came forward to shake their hands.

"Dad told us a little about the case he's working on for you," Frank explained. "And while we were in Los Angeles, we came across a mystery that may tie in with it."

A shadow of concern clouded over Eric Barnes's face.

Turn to page 113.

16

The Hardys rushed to their rented white sedan, which was parked in front of Lila Lewis's mansion. Frank jumped in behind the wheel and started the engine, while Joe got into the passenger seat.

"Let's go!" he exclaimed as the car shot off after the gardener's brown Volkswagen.

Frank trailed Peter through the exclusive Los Angeles suburb to a freeway that led west to the Pacific Ocean.

"We're headed toward the waterfront," the dark-haired detective surmised as he caught a whiff of the ocean air. "And I bet Peter isn't taking off work in the middle of the day to go surfing."

Just then, the Volkswagen exited from the freeway. Frank swung their rented sedan onto the ramp as well and trailed Peter through several blocks of warehouses along the docks.

Suddenly, the suspect stopped in front of a dilapidated building. Frank pulled into a nearby loading bay.

"You're right." Joe chuckled. "He's not going surfing!"

Turn to page 19.

"If Barlow hasn't shown up for work, he may be in Los Angeles," Frank continued. "In fact, he might be using the Lewis mansión for clandestine activities while his aunt is out of town."

17

"Mr. Barnes," Joe asked, "could we have a look at Barlow's personnel file before we leave? It may give us some information to work on."

"I'll call down for it right now," the executive answered.

While the two detectives waited for the file to be brought in, Eric Barnes described the company's security measures to them.

"There are several levels of security built into our main data bank," he explained. "Secret passwords are needed to gain access at each level. Unfortunately, Barlow has the key word to obtain any kind of information he wants."

Just then, a secretary walked into the room, carrying a gray folder.

"Here's his confidential record," Mr. Barnes announced.

Turn to page 18.

18

"Thank you," Frank responded as he flipped open the file.

"Joe, look at that picture!" he exclaimed.

"Barlow fits the description of the man Jill saw fleeing from the mansion last night," Joe confirmed. "Curly hair must run in the family."

"And here's a Los Angeles address he gave as one of his residences," Frank added.

The detectives carefully perused the rest of the file. Then they stood up to say good-bye to Eric Barnes.

"We'll keep in touch with you about any developments," Joe assured him. "I think we may be on to a solution to our mystery and your problem."

After the boys left the Tri-Tech complex, they had dinner and found a hotel to spend the night. Early the following morning, they returned to Los Angeles.

Turn to page 25.

The Hardys jumped out of the car and cautiously walked toward the warehouse Peter had entered. It jutted out on a dock over the water.

"Sure is lonely around here," Joe whispered, noticing that the area appeared to be deserted.

Frank nodded. "Come on," he urged, climbing the steps of the dock. "We'll circle around back."

The two detectives crept along the rotting boards of the structure until they reached a door at the rear. Frank put his shoulder into it and turned the rusty knob. It shuddered open, and they slipped into a dark, musty room.

Frank raised a finger to his lips, signaling Joe to be still. The sound of voices was filtering through from the other side of the wall. The sleuths pressed their ears against it.

"I've got the money!" someone was saying. "Those rich people are willing to pay a bundle to get illegal aliens to work for them."

"Good work, Peter," a second voice exclaimed. "This makes smuggling those people in from Mexico all worthwhile."

Turn to page 20.

20

"Where are you keeping them?" Peter asked.

"They're hiding in my house," his accomplice answered. "I'll drive them over to you tonight."

"Okay, let's split this cash and get out of here!" the gardener declared. "This place gives me the creeps."

After a long silence, Joe whispered to his brother, "We'd better do something before they get away!"

"You're right," Frank agreed. "Let's make our move."

The sleuths crept toward a door that led into the next room. With a powerful push, Joe slammed it open. The two criminals looked up with startled eyes.

"Get out of here!" Peter yelled to his partner, and made a dash for the front door.

Frank and Joe rushed across the long room in pursuit. When they reached the dock, both stopped dead in their tracks. Peter was jumping into his car. The other man had just leapt into a motorboat tied up nearby!

If you think the Hardys should pursue Peter, turn to page 39.

If you think they should stop the motorboat, turn to page 74.

Jill caught up with Nancy and handed her a ring with keys to all the buildings on Miss Lewis's estate, and the two girls walked toward the gardener's cottage.

21

"We have to be careful," the girl detective warned her friend. "I don't want Peter to know we've searched his rooms."

She tried several keys until she found the one that opened the lock. Then she and Jill quickly slipped inside, shutting the door behind them.

They split up to speed the search.

"Hmm, there's not much here," Nancy whispered as she opened a closet in the kitchen.

Just then, Jill called out from the bedroom. "Nancy, look at this!"

The detective joined her friend, who was pointing to an old-fashioned trunk under a window.

"It seems like a good place to hide something," Jill said.

Nancy nodded and stooped down to undo the brass latch.

Turn to page 24.

22

"The question is . . . where can we find him now?" Frank muttered thoughtfully as he searched through piles of computer printouts on Barlow's desk.

Joe noticed an answering device attached to the researcher's telephone. He pushed the rewind button, then pressed the one to start the tape. The recorder gave out several messages of no interest, but then a voice with a foreign accent came on.

"Confirming rendezvous," it said. "Pacifica Yacht Club, 7:00 P.M."

The message ended abruptly with the click of a telephone receiver.

"We're on to something!" Joe said excitedly. "Barlow is supposed to meet someone at a yacht club at 7:00."

"We don't know if it's tonight, though," Frank cautioned.

Just then, a telephone on Barlow's desk rang shrilly. Joe picked it up to hear Eric Barnes's agitated voice on the other end.

Turn to page 26.

A few moments later, Jill handed Nancy the keys to her car. "Where will you go?" she inquired.

"I've decided to go to Jack Turner's office at the movie studio," the young sleuth replied.

"Meanwhile, we'll head up north to the computer firm Dad is working for," Frank announced.

Joe asked Jill Blake for her telephone number so that he and Frank could keep in touch with her and Nancy, and gave her the number of the firm the boys would be visiting. Then the detectives walked out to the front of the house. Nancy got into Jill's Porsche, while Frank and Joe went to their rental car.

The Hardys left right away, but Nancy studied a map of the Los Angeles area first. She decided upon her route to the movie lot and then took off, waving good-bye to Jill.

Turn to page 27.

24

When she lifted up the heavy lid, the girls saw a glimmering gold vase lying on a towel inside. At that moment, the door to the cottage creaked open. Jill stared at her friend with alarm in her eyes.

If you think the girls should try to hide, turn to page 32.
If you think they should stand their ground, turn to page 50.

On the way, they discussed the case of Craig Barlow.

"The computer industry has been plagued with high-tech crime," Frank said. "Barlow may be one of the guys who saw the chance to make an easy million."

"But who could he be working for?" Joe asked.

"Foreign competition, other computer researchers, any number of people," Frank replied. "Dad mentioned to me that the field is growing so fast that companies will do anything to stay on top of the market."

When they reached the outskirts of the metropolitan Los Angeles area, the brothers discussed their next move.

"I took down the L.A. address from Barlow's file," Frank said. "We could swing by there and see if he's around."

"Or we could go back to the Lewis place," Joe added. "We should do a thorough search of the house. Also, Nancy should be informed about our progress."

If you think the detectives should go to the Lewis mansion,
turn to page 34.
If you want them to stop at Barlow's Los Angeles address,
turn to page 66.

26

"I just received word that Barlow has gained entry to the main data bank from outside the complex. He could be making a printout of our top-secret programs!"

"Is there any way you can stop him?" Joe asked.

"I've put a trace on the call," the executive answered. "We may be able to locate where it's coming from."

"And we just listened to a message on his answering machine," Joe explained. "He's supposed to meet someone at the Pacifica Yacht Club at 7:00. If that's tonight, we'll have to go there right away!"

"It's not too far from here on the San Francisco Bay," Barnes said. "Let me know what you're planning to do. One way or another, we have to stop Barlow!"

If you think the Hardys should drive to the yacht club for the rendezvous, turn to page 36.
If you think they should wait for Barlow's computer line to be traced, turn to page 46.

Forty minutes later, the girl detective drove through the main gate of one of California's major film studios.

"I'd like to see Mr. Jack Turner," she explained to the guard who stopped her. "Could you tell me where to find him?"

"Mr. Turner?" the man questioned, searching through a directory of employees. "He works in the editing unit of Studio B. I'll mark it for you on this map of the grounds."

"Thank you," Nancy said, and took the map.

After parking the car, she walked toward Studio B and looked curiously at the make-believe world around her. She passed a film crew in front of a set that looked like a European street corner. But the buildings were only facades propped up by boards. Farther on, she saw a group of workmen rearranging huge boulders that seemed to weigh only ounces.

Finally, the young sleuth arrived at Studio B and approached the receptionist in the lobby.

"I'm here to see Mr. Turner," she announced.

"I'm sorry, but he's left already," the young woman responded politely. "He often comes back to his office in the evening, though. Shall I leave a message for him?"

Turn to page 28.

28

Nancy hesitated for a moment. "Please tell Mr. Turner that Nancy Drew would like to speak to him as soon as possible," she said finally.

She was just about to tell the receptionist how she could be reached when she noticed a young man in his late twenties approaching her.

"Are you Nancy Drew, the amateur detective?" he inquired eagerly.

"Yes, I am," she answered.

Turn to page 48.

The left fork seems to go down to the beach, Nancy thought. *I'll try that.*

After a short drive, she came to a dead end. She saw the red Triumph parked in a lot with other cars and several large vans marked with the movie studio's name.

As Nancy got out of her Porsche, she noticed a cluster of people standing on the beach.

They're shooting a movie on location here, she deduced, then saw Jack Turner in the group. He was handing a briefcase to a man sitting in a director's chair.

The young sleuth hurried across the beach to the movie crew. Just as she approached, she heard the director call out, "Scene forty-one, first take!"

Nancy watched with fascination as a young actor in an expensive dinner jacket ran toward the ocean. He was singing a song as he waded out into the water. Then, with a dramatic gesture, he popped open the briefcase that Jack Turner had given the director. Hundreds of dollar bills flew up in the air and were scattered over the waves.

Turn to page 30.

30

The actor let out a wild laugh and threw more money into the breeze.

"Okay, cut!" the director yelled. "That was a good take! We'll print it."

Nancy walked toward Jack Turner as several crew members went down to clean up the beach.

"Hello," she said to the young man. "I'm Nancy Drew, a friend of Jill Blake's."

"Jack Turner," he responded with a smile. "Did you enjoy the scene?"

"Yes, very much," Nancy said. "You know, Jill told me about a briefcase full of money she had seen at Lila Lewis's place last night. We thought it was quite a mystery."

"I almost left it at my grandmother's," Jack Turner explained. "I had to go back to get it. The money was fake, of course."

"Of course," Nancy repeated with a smile.

Turn to page 38.

The next day, Nancy sat in the Blakes' house talking to Frank, Joe, and Jill. The Hardys had returned from Silicon Valley after learning that the computer chip they had found was worthless.

31

"You actually locked those guys in the dungeon?" Joe asked gleefully.

"That's right," Nancy answered with a mischievous grin. "Then I went to get Todd Hanson, a detective on the lot. Turner confessed that he was being paid off by an enemy of one of the studio's directors. They're both in a real jail cell now."

"What an exciting story!" Jill Blake exclaimed.

"Maybe they'll make it into a movie," Frank added with a laugh.

END

32

Nancy closed the trunk and pulled Jill toward the bedroom closet.

The two girls slipped inside and left the door open just a little bit. Nancy peered through the crack.

She spied a young man moving across the room toward the trunk under the window. Because of his long, curly hair, she thought the intruder was Jack Turner. But when she gave Jill a chance to look, the girl quietly shook her head, indicating that he was a stranger.

The young man quickly threw open the lid of the trunk and let out a satisfied laugh when he saw its contents. He picked up the shiny gold vase and several pieces of jewelry that had obviously been hidden under the towel.

"Peter was busy last night, I see," he muttered to himself gleefully. Then he stuffed the valuable goods into a knapsack he was carrying and walked out of the room. A moment later, he slammed the front door, signaling to the girls that he had left the cottage.

Turn to page 59.

34 "I have a hunch that Barlow might be working out of his aunt's house," Joe continued. "It would be a great cover for illegal activities. He probably didn't know that Lila Lewis had asked Jill to keep an eye on it."

"Okay, let's drive back there," his brother agreed.

Within an hour, the Hardys arrived at the Blakes' and told the two girls about Craig Barlow.

"We'd like to investigate Miss Lewis's home thoroughly, if it's all right with you," Joe said to Jill.

"Sure. I was planning to go over to check on things anyway," the dark-haired girl replied.

The three sleuths followed Jill to her neighbor's property.

"Let's start on the top floor," Frank suggested, "and work our way down. This place is so huge it could take us hours to open every door."

The friends climbed the wide curved staircase that led upstairs. In the hallway at the top, they agreed to split up.

"Jill and I will check the rooms to the left," Nancy announced.

"We'll go to the right," Frank added.

If you want to follow Nancy, turn to page 35.
If you want to follow the Hardys, turn to page 43.

The titian-blonde sleuth carefully searched the first bedroom but found nothing. Jill trailed behind as Nancy opened the second door to the left.

35

The moment the girl detective entered the room, a rough hand clamped over her mouth, and strong arms pulled her inside. Nancy stared in shock at her attacker as he slammed shut the door and locked it.

"What are you doing here?" the man hissed.

"You must be Craig Barlow," she said in a controlled voice.

"This is my aunt's house," Barlow snarled. "I could have you arrested for trespassing."

"Then why don't you call the police?" she countered.

Rage clouded the man's handsome face.

"Who else is here with you?" he demanded.

Turn to page 40.

36

"My hunch is that the meeting at the yacht club is tonight," Joe said. "We could nab both Barlow and his partner if we got there on time."

"Okay, let's tell Eric Barnes where we're going and then take off," Frank added.

The Hardys rushed from the research section to the vice-president's office and informed him of their plans. He gave them directions to the yacht club, and they set off immediately.

The rush-hour traffic slowed them down to a crawl. Frank nervously checked his watch every ten minutes as the time came nearer and nearer to 7:00. At five minutes before the hour, the boys finally pulled up to the exclusive club.

"Look, Joe," the older Hardy exclaimed as they were getting out of the car. "Look at that guy walking down the dock."

"I see him all right," his brother replied. "It's Craig Barlow!"

Turn to page 42.

When the young people had returned to the Blake house, Nancy studied a map of the Los Angeles area.

"Jack Turner lives on the way to the movie studio," she announced. "I'll stop by there first."

"We'd better start out right away for the computer headquarters," Frank said.

"We'll call you tonight, Nancy," Joe added, "to keep in touch about our investigations."

The three sleuths went out to the cars and waved good-bye to Jill Blake. Nancy drove away in her friend's green Porsche and headed northeast to Jack Turner's house.

Turn to page 51.

38

Later that afternoon, Nancy dove into the cool water of the Blakes' swimming pool. She surfaced and swam over to the edge where Jill was sitting.

"I'm so happy that Jack is innocent!" the young girl exclaimed.

"Wait till Frank and Joe hear about this!" Nancy said, shaking drops out of her titian-blonde hair. "They'll wish they had followed the lead I did."

"I hope they'll be back by tomorrow," Jill said. "We'll have a pool party and celebrate."

"Maybe we can even invite Jack Turner!" Nancy said with a grin, then dove back into the clear blue water.

END

39

"We're too late to catch the boat," Frank moaned with dismay as they watched the vessel pull away from the dock. "But I got its registration number. Let's try to grab Peter now!"

The Hardys sped down the dock to the brown car. Joe grabbed the door handle on the passenger's side just as Peter got the engine, which had stalled several times, to start. The blond sleuth swung open the door and jumped inside. Peter had his foot on the gas. Joe twisted the wheel to the right and forced the driver to come to a screeching halt inches away from the water.

"Don't move!" he threatened the gardener. "We'll have the police here in a few minutes. They'll be very interested in the story we just overheard."

Turn to page 84.

40

Nancy attempted to stall Barlow's questioning when she suddenly spotted Joe Hardy outside the window, standing on a ledge. He was trying to get into the room to rescue her. The girl detective knew she had to keep Barlow from seeing her friend.

"I'm curious about the money you had here last night," she went on, knowing that would get his full attention. "Where did it come from?"

"How do you know about that?" the young man demanded nervously.

"I . . . I . . . ," Nancy began and then started to cough loudly. Joe was pushing open the window from the outside, and she hoped to cover any noise he might make.

"Answer me!" Barlow demanded.

A second later, the younger Hardy jumped into the room and wrestled Barlow to the floor. Nancy immediately unlocked the door and flung it open. Frank and Jill rushed in with worried expressions on their faces.

Turn to page 41.

"Okay, Barlow, it's time for you to explain some things," Joe said in a threatening voice. "We're calling the police!"

Just then, a door creaked open on the ground floor. Frank ran with Nancy to the head of the staircase. A man in dark sunglasses was walking into the living room, carrying a briefcase.

"Get out of here, Taylor," Craig Barlow suddenly yelled.

The man stopped in his tracks, then rushed for the door. Frank sprinted down the steps toward him. The dark-haired detective managed to make a tackle in the hallway.

"Call the police, Nancy!" he called out as he struggled with the man. "We need help!"

Turn to page 63.

42

The young detectives ran toward the dock, which was lined on both sides by expensive private yachts. Barlow was several yards ahead of them, confidently swinging a thick briefcase by his side.

"Just act as if you know what you're doing," Frank whispered to Joe as the suspect suddenly turned around and looked at them. The two boys knelt down and pretended to inspect the moorings of one of the boats.

Barlow walked rapidly on until he came to a beautiful blue-and-white sailing yacht. The Hardys watched as he jumped on board and then climbed through the hatch to go below deck.

"Come on," Frank murmured, "let's follow him."

"I wonder why nobody else is around?" Joe asked, glancing at the empty boats.

"They're all having dinner at the club," Frank guessed. "But someone may be on that blue-and-white sailboat."

The brothers crept toward the yacht, straining their ears to hear the sound of voices.

"Let's go aboard," Frank finally decided. "We've got to have real evidence that Barlow is making an illegal deal."

Turn to page 44.

Frank and Joe went down the hallway to the right. They checked the two bedrooms there, but noticed nothing suspicious.

43

"Let's get back to Nancy and Jill," Joe suggested. "Maybe they've found something."

Just then, Jill Blake rushed up with a look of alarm on her face.

"We've got to help Nancy!" she said excitedly. "Craig Barlow caught her snooping."

Turn to page 40.

44

Silently, the Hardys stepped onto the boat, taking cover behind the rigging of the mainsail.

"Listen!" Joe whispered a moment later.

They could hear Barlow talking with another man, who had a thick foreign accent. The research engineer was assuring his partner that all the information he had promised him was in the printout.

"Okay, we've got the goods on Barlow," Frank said. "Now we have to make sure that other guy doesn't get away with Tri-Tech's secrets."

"I say we should make a surprise attack on them," Joe said confidently.

Frank shook his head. "I have another idea," he said.

If you want to follow Joe's suggestion, turn to page 45.
If you want to hear Frank's idea, turn to page 52.

"Come on, it's two against two," Joe said insistently. "We can handle them."

"Oh . . . all right," Frank finally agreed. The brothers crept up to the hatch and readied themselves for a surprise attack.

"I'll go down first," Joe whispered. "Follow close behind."

But as he plunged down the stairs, he suddenly felt a devastating blow on the back of his head. He fell forward, knocked unconscious!

"Joc, what happened?" Frank called out. Then he, too, was hit and sank into darkness!

45

Turn to page 78.

46

"I think we should wait for Barlow to be traced," Frank suggested.

"Okay," Joe agreed. "Let's go back to Mr. Barnes. He'll be the first to know where Barlow is calling from."

The brothers left the research section, then headed back to the vice-president's office.

"We know he's in the San Jose area," Eric Barnes announced as they walked in. "If he stays on long enough, we'll be able to pinpoint his location."

The executive was holding a telephone to his ear, listening to information being given to him on the other end. Everyone in the room waited with hushed anticipation.

"Great!" Barnes suddenly exclaimed. "You got it. That's two hundred seventy Beach Road, San Jose."

Frank quickly jotted down the address on a notepad he carried with him.

"San Jose is about an hour from here," the vice-president explained. "If you hurry, you may be able to recover the information he's taken from the computer."

"We're on our way," Joe called out as the Hardys rushed for the door.

Turn to page 47.

Joe directed his brother from a detailed map of the area. Once they reached San Jose, they wove through the rush-hour traffic for a while until they reached their destination.

"There it is," the younger Hardy exclaimed, "Beach Road."

Frank turned left on the narrow street, which was lined with quaint wooden houses, and braked to a stop in front of number 270.

"Look, a car is still in the driveway," he said. "We must have made it in time."

"I wonder how many people are inside?" Joe questioned. "This could be more than we can handle."

"We'll check out the place first," Frank decided. "You circle around to the left, and I'll take the right side."

Turn to page 53.

48

"My name is Todd Hanson," the young man said, reaching out to shake her hand. "I'm a detective on the security force of the studio. I've followed your career with great interest. Are you here on a case, by any chance?"

"Yes, I am," Nancy replied in a low voice. "Could we talk outside?"

Todd Hanson followed the young sleuth out of Studio B, curiosity shining in his eyes.

"I'm here to see Jack Turner," Nancy explained after they had left the building. "I wanted to ask him about something a friend of mine found in his grandmother's house. My friend thought she saw Jack leave the house last night, so he may know something about it."

"Well," Todd Hanson said, "he'll probably be back later. Can you return this evening?"

Turn to page 49.

"Of course," the girl detective replied.

"I'll write up a pass for you," Todd offered. "I'll be here myself tonight."

"Thank you very much," Nancy said as she took the pass he had filled out.

"Perhaps we'll meet again." Todd grinned. "In the meantime, why don't you take the studio tour? It will acquaint you with the grounds, and it's lots of fun!"

"Good idea," Nancy said. "I'll do that." She waved good-bye to the friendly detective and spent the next two hours enjoying herself, looking at sets and listening to stories about the latest movies being shot in the studio.

Turn to page 68.

50

Nancy calmly stood her ground as a young man with long, curly hair stepped into the bedroom of the cottage.

"What are you doing here?" he demanded arrogantly.

"I was just about to ask you the same question," the young sleuth replied.

"I'm Peter's friend," the intruder announced. "And he wouldn't like you snooping around."

"As a matter of fact," Nancy said, deciding to call his bluff, "there are some interesting items in that trunk over there. I wonder where Peter could have found them."

A look of anger flashed across the young man's face. He reached into his pocket and pulled out a sharp-bladed knife.

"You'll be sorry you ever came here," he threatened.

Turn to page 93.

Thirty minutes later, the girl detective pulled up in front of an attractive bungalow set on a hillside above Los Angeles. She was about to open her car door when she saw a handsome young man with long, curly hair come out. He spoke a few words to a woman in a maid's uniform before bounding down the steps to a red sports car.

Nancy quickly took a map and pretended to study it so Turner would not see her face.

"I could follow him and see where's he's going," she murmured to herself. "On the other hand, this may be a good chance to get information from the maid."

If you want Nancy to follow the red sports car, turn to page 58.
If you think she should talk to Turner's maid, turn to page 69.

52

"We'll have to work fast," Frank began. "If we can shut that hatch and tie the two handles together, they'll never be able to get out. Then we can call the police."

"Brilliant!" Joe exclaimed. "Here's some rope we can use."

The brothers stole over to the hatch. Frank suddenly slammed down both its doors; a second later, Joe was twisting rope around the handles in secure knots.

"Run and call the authorities," Frank yelled to Joe as angry fists began to pound on the door. "I'll hold the lid on things here!"

Turn to page 77.

The brothers crept up the stairs leading to a deck that ran along the outside of the house. Joe turned left, then rounded the first corner. Drifting through a window were the voices of a young man and woman. The sleuth pressed his body against the side of the house and listened.

"What if they catch us, Craig?" the woman said nervously.

"Don't worry," Barlow replied. "We'll be in Mexico before Tri-Tech knows they've lost their top secrets. All we have to do now is pick up our final payoff at the yacht club. Then we can retire for life."

Joe moved his head nearer the window and peeked inside. He saw an array of sophisticated computer hardware in the room.

At that moment, the young woman turned toward him. He jerked his head away but was a second too late.

"Craig, somebody's out there!" she cried.

Joe ran to the back door of the house and almost smacked into Frank as he rounded the corner.

"What happened?" his brother demanded.

"They saw me," Joe panted.

"We'd better hurry to the front!" Frank exclaimed. "They'll probably try to get away!"

Turn to page 54.

54

When the Hardys reached the driveway, they saw Barlow and his girlfriend running to the car that was parked there. Barlow was carrying a heavy case that slowed his pace.

Frank and Joe sprinted after the couple, overtaking them a few seconds later. The detectives tackled the suspect, then pinned his arms behind his back. The girl began to cry but didn't make an attempt to get away.

"What do you want?" Barlow asked the Hardys with an edge of panic in his voice.

"Eric Barnes sent us from Tri-Tech," Joe answered. "You weren't as smart as you thought, Barlow. You dropped a computer chip at your aunt's house last night before you got away with your payoff."

"And if you want to be smart now," Frank added, "you'll lead the police to your contact at the yacht club."

"You win," Barlow moaned. "I'll do whatever you say."

Turn to page 97.

56

"That stolen print could cost the studio thousands!" Todd Hanson exclaimed. "Try to stay with the crook who has it. I'll send a police car after you."

"I'm driving a green Porsche," the young sleuth said. "The license number is 76ONJI."

"Good. I'll alert the Los Angeles authorities immediately," the studio detective said. "I'll tell them to have someone meet us at the Lewis home as well. And thanks, Nancy. You've been very helpful."

Nancy hung up the phone and cautiously stepped into the hallway. A moment later, she slipped out of the building and surveyed the parking lot. Jack Turner was climbing into a red sports car; the man with the stolen film was driving away in an expensive-looking black sedan.

As soon as both cars had left the parking lot, Nancy ran to Jill's Porsche, switched on the engine, and drove to the gate. She caught a glimpse of the crook as the black sedan turned right onto a main avenue, and followed a safe distance behind him.

The lights of Los Angeles glimmered below as she trailed the man at a steady speed. He was heading west, toward a large thoroughfare.

"I hope the police catch up soon," Nancy murmured anxiously to herself, concerned that she might lose the sedan on the busy freeway.

Turn to page 57.

From page 56

Several minutes later, the girl detective breathed a sigh of relief. The flashing red lights of a cruiser were rapidly approaching her from behind. Nancy pulled to the side of the road and rolled down her window as the police car came up beside her.

"The thief with the print is in a black Lincoln, license number 842MLO," she called out.

"Thanks, Miss Drew," the officer responded. "We'll pick him up right away."

As the cruiser moved on, Nancy headed back to the studio to meet Todd Hanson. They had less than an hour to surprise Jack Turner at his grandmother's house.

Turn to page 86.

58

Nancy watched Jack Turner's sports car pull away down the shady street.

"I'll follow him," she decided. "I can always stop back here later."

The girl detective switched on the engine of her friend's Porsche and drove off after the red Triumph.

Turner headed west on a freeway that led to the California coast. Nancy managed to tail him through the heavy Los Angeles traffic.

"He isn't going to the movie studio, that's for sure," the young sleuth murmured as she saw the sports car exit on a ramp marked Huntington Beach.

After several more miles, she suddenly smelled the salty tang of ocean air. The road had narrowed, and a few cars had come between Turner and her. As she rounded a curve, Nancy realized that he had escaped from her view. A fork lay ahead. She had to decide whether she should turn left or right!

If you want Nancy to go left, turn to page 29.
If you want her to go right, turn to page 64.

"We've got to follow him!" Nancy urged her friend.

The two girls hurried to the door and caught sight of the young man walking hastily through the back of the garden.

"He's headed toward the cliffside that leads down to a road behind the house," Jill explained.

"Come on," the titian-blonde sleuth murmured as they began to pursue the intruder.

By the time the girls reached the steep incline, the young man was scrambling down it.

"We're going to lose him!" Nancy said with frustration as she and Jill picked their way through the thick trees and bushes. A second later, they noticed a brown Volkswagen waiting by the road at the bottom of the hill.

"That's Peter's car," Jill announced.

Nancy watched nervously as the thief reached the small vehicle. He opened the passenger door and climbed in.

Turn to page 60.

60

Just then, Nancy saw the Hardys slowly approaching the car from the rear. The young detective quickened her descent and ran into view of her friends.

"Stop them!" she yelled.

Instantly, Frank and Joe rushed to the car and pulled open both doors. The gardener and his accomplice were sitting inside, inspecting the expensive items that had been in the trunk. Neither of the suspects had heard Nancy's call, and they stared dumbfounded at the Hardys.

"You have some explanations to make, Peter," Frank declared. "You and your friend can give them to the police."

"I'll run to the house and call them," Jill offered.

"And we'll stay right here to make sure these crooks don't get away," Joe added.

Turn to page 72.

Frank hurried toward Gate 32, slowing down only to pass through the airport's security check. When he arrived, he was dismayed to see that all the passengers had already boarded the plane for Tokyo.

61

"I'm too late!" he muttered with disappointment.

Frank glanced around the lobby and noticed a red security phone on the wall. Quickly, he approached it, then dialed the number on the box.

"Hello, could I speak with the security chief?" he asked.

A man who identified himself as Tom Ackerman came on the line. Frank gave his name and explained the situation.

"Are you Fenton Hardy's son, by any chance?" the chief inquired.

"Yes, I am," the sleuth answered. "Do you know my father?"

"We worked together years ago," Mr. Ackerman replied. "What can I do to help you?"

Breathing a deep sigh of relief, Frank requested that security officers check to see if Craig Barlow was on the flight to Japan.

Turn to page 62.

62

"I'll contact the pilot to hold the plane," the chief said. "And I'll come in person to investigate. Stay where you are. I'll meet you there."

Just as Frank hung up the phone, his brother ran up.

"I watched every passenger get on the flight to Hong Kong," the younger Hardy reported. "And I didn't see Craig Barlow."

"Well, we'll soon know whether he's going to Tokyo," Frank said. "The chief of security is holding the aircraft."

Minutes later, Tom Ackerman arrived with the news that Barlow *was* on the jet for Tokyo. The two brothers accompanied him through the boarding gate and into the plane. Frank saw the suspect sitting in an aisle seat near the back. The security chief immediately requested that the young man deplane.

"What's going on here!" Barlow demanded, gripping his briefcase tightly.

"That's what we plan to find out," Joe replied as the four walked into the terminal.

Turn to page 76.

By the time the police arrived, the two suspects were securely tied up. Nancy had opened the briefcase and found stacks of bills inside. Joe had searched the upstairs bedroom and discovered a cache of computer parts, while Frank got in touch with Eric Barnes of Tri-Tech Industries.

63

As the officers led the two men away, he put down the phone.

"Mr. Barnes is coming to Los Angeles to press charges," he explained to the others. "He just discovered valuable computer hardware missing from his research section. Barlow must have stolen it to sell to a competitor."

"He was being paid pretty well," Joe put in. "There was twenty-five thousand dollars in that briefcase!"

"I was lucky I didn't bump into Craig Barlow the other night," Jill added with a shudder.

"This mansion has been anything but deserted lately," Nancy said with a sigh. "But I'm ready to desert it now!"

END

64

Nancy peered down the fork to the right. Some distance away, she saw a gray clapboard building. She also noticed Jack Turner's car pulling up next to a yellow car in front of the building.

The young sleuth followed him, then parked in a stand of trees behind the building. She hopped out of the Porsche and cautiously crept up to the dilapidated structure. Coming closer, she heard voices on the front porch. She cast a quick glance around the nearest corner and saw Jack Turner and a tough-looking man wearing dark sunglasses.

"Here's the money," Turner was saying in a nervous voice. "It's everything I owe you."

Nancy heard a briefcase snap open. Then there was a short silence.

"Two thousand dollars," the other man sneered in a nasty voice. "This should teach a loser like you not to gamble anymore."

"I've learned my lesson," Turner responded. "Now leave me alone."

"Fine with me," the other man snarled. "You're just lucky you have rich relatives!"

Turn to page 65.

From page 64

Nancy heard the steps of the old building creak. When she peeked out again, the yellow car was pulling away. Jack Turner stood alone on the porch. The girl detective waited a minute and then walked into sight.

"Mr. Turner," she said, "I'm Nancy Drew, a friend of Jill Blake's. Jill told me about a briefcase full of money she saw in Lila Lewis's house last night. Since I'm an amateur detective, I followed you to find out what the mystery was. I overheard your conversation just now."

A look of embarrassment came over Turner's face.

"I'm afraid my grandmother had to bail me out of a dangerous situation," he said. "She left me the money before she went to Europe. I had to promise her I'd never gamble again."

"I'm happy to hear that," Nancy said with a kind smile. "We thought you might be in even worse trouble."

"This was bad enough!" Turner exclaimed. "But it's all over now."

They spoke for a few more minutes, then said good-bye and left.

Turn to page 83.

66

"Check out Barlow's street on the map," Frank requested. "We'll see if he's staying at that address."

Joe directed his brother to a condominium development on a hill that overlooked the Pacific Ocean.

"Not a bad place to live," Frank commented, and parked their car.

"Not bad at all," Joe added as he noticed several young women in bikinis lounging around a pool. The blond sleuth approached one of the sunbathers.

"We're looking for Craig Barlow," he said. "Do you know if he still lives here?"

"He's here on weekends sometimes," the girl replied with a smile. "And I saw him around during the last two days."

"Which is his apartment?" Frank inquired.

"Oh, you won't find him now," the girl answered. "He just pulled away . . . about half an hour ago . . . in an airport limousine."

"Do you know where he was going?" Joe asked.

Turn to page 67.

"Well, not exactly . . . ," the girl said. "But I did chat with him for a minute, and I saw he was holding a ticket from Northwest Orient Airlines."

"Thanks, thanks a lot!" Frank called out, then he and Joe rushed back to their car.

"We have to get to the airport fast!" the younger Hardy exclaimed. "It looks like Barlow may be leaving the country!"

Turn to page 117.

From page 49

68

After the tour, Nancy had dinner in a nearby Mexican restaurant. When she had finished, she returned to the lot and showed her pass to the guard at the main gate. He admitted her without asking any questions, and she parked Jill's Porsche near Studio B.

This place is so different at night, she thought as she glanced at the sets. In the fading light, the area had taken on an eerie, ghostly look.

The girl detective walked toward the entrance of the building where Jack Turner worked. She hoped to find him inside and catch him off guard with her questions. She was about to open the door when she saw a man with long, curly hair disappear around the corner of one of the sets. He was carrying a briefcase!

The sleuth paused a moment to decide what she should do. She could go into the studio and try to find Turner. Or she could follow the man she had just seen.

If you think Nancy should go into the studio, turn to page 81.
If you think she should follow the mysterious man, turn to page 94.

Nancy decided to stay at Turner's bungalow and talk to the maid.

The titian-blonde sleuth waited until the red sports car was well out of sight. Then she walked up the steps to where the maid was shaking out an expensive rug.

"Hello," Nancy said in a polite tone. "Is Mr. Turner home?"

"No. I'm afraid you just missed him," the plump red-haired woman replied. "He's gone off to see that young actress again."

"Oh, that's too bad," Nancy said and glanced through the open door of the bungalow. Inside, she saw several photographs of famous movie stars on the walls. To her surprise, the picture of Jennifer Quinn, a rising starlet, had a dart stuck in it.

"Could I find Mr. Turner at Miss Quinn's house?" she asked on a hunch.

Turn to page 70.

70

"Yes, that's where he was going," the maid answered. "Her home is just a short drive from here, on Blue Canyon."

"I can't recall the address," the sleuth said coyly.

"Number two forty-eight," the plump woman volunteered.

"Thank you for your help," Nancy said, and turned to walk back to her car. "And have a nice day."

"You too, dearie," the maid called out as she went into the bungalow.

"Jack Turner apparently has a grudge against Jennifer Quinn," Nancy murmured to herself as she switched on the engine. "I'd better go to Blue Canyon right away."

She checked her map, then headed for the young starlet's address. Fifteen minutes later, she pulled up in front of a contemporary white stucco house. Turner's Triumph was parked in the driveway.

The girl detective left her car and quietly walked up the terraced front steps. Before knocking on the door, she surveyed the property. A flagstone walk led around the side of the house. She decided to see where it would take her and followed it.

Turn to page 71.

Thick shrubs hid Nancy as she came to the corner of the house. Glancing cautiously into the backyard, she saw Jack Turner talking to a beautiful young woman. Nancy immediately recognized Jennifer Quinn's long blonde hair and exquisite features.

"I want another two thousand dollars next month," the young man was saying to the actress in a threatening voice.

71

Turn to page 91.

72

About fifteen minutes later, the three young detectives and Jill, who had just come back from the house, watched as the police took away the gardener and his curly-haired partner.

"The authorities received theft reports on every item those crooks have taken," Frank explained. "It seems that Peter has been stealing valuables from the wealthy residents around here. The other guy was acting as his fence."

"Then the money I saw last night must have been Peter's payoff for stolen goods," Jill said.

"That's right," Joe responded. "You were lucky that you left the house when you did. You might have been hurt."

"I'm so relieved Jack Turner wasn't involved in this," Jill sighed. "I shouldn't have suspected him."

"This computer chip is still a mystery," Frank said as he took the object from his pocket. "But we'll have to wait for Miss Lewis to explain it."

"I think we've solved enough mysteries for one day!" Nancy exclaimed with a laugh. "I don't know about you, but I'm ready for a swim and some California sunshine!"

END

"By the way," Jill said, "Jack asked me about a computer chip he had lost. So that mystery's cleared up, too."

"Case closed!" Joe said with a triumphant grin. Then he groaned with pain and added, "It only hurts when I smile!"

END

73

74

"We know where we can find Peter later," Frank said. "Let's stop that guy in the water."

The engine of the boat roared to life, and the craft began to pull away from the dock just as Frank and Joe reached it.

"Jump!" Joe yelled, leaping into the back of the boat. A second later, Frank followed, just clearing the edge of the stern. The man at the wheel turned around with a look of panic on his face. He gunned the motor, then pulled a knife as Joe rushed toward him.

The younger Hardy stopped short at the sight of the weapon. The criminal slashed the air in front of the sleuth, forcing him to the edge of the boat. Joe tried to protect himself, but his burly opponent was too fast. He reached out his other arm and knocked Joe into the choppy waves of the Pacific!

Turn to page 79.

76

"I've given the pilot clearance for takeoff," Mr. Ackerman said as he ushered the suspect into a security office. "Now, Mr. Barlow, explain to us what's in your briefcase."

"I'm not telling you a thing," the young man replied in a surly voice. "I want to call my lawyer!"

"And we'll call Eric Barnes at Tri-Tech Industries," Joe shot back. "He's very interested in the computer chip you dropped two nights ago in your aunt's house."

A look of shock came over the young man's handsome face.

"All right," he said, "I don't want to go to jail! What do you need to know?"

Turn to page 96.

The next day, Frank and Joe leaned back against their leather chairs in the Pacifica Yacht Club. They had just finished a complimentary dinner there with Nancy and Jill.

"You mean you actually stood on that hatch until the police arrived?" Nancy asked with a smile.

"Barlow and his partner got a big surprise when I finally let them out," Frank explained. "They walked right into the arms of the authorities."

"The partner was a foreign competitor of Tri-Tech Industries," Joe went on. "He had planned on setting sail tomorrow . . . taking the top-secret printouts with him."

"Barlow admitted to being in his aunt's house the day before yesterday," Frank added. "Jill walked into the middle of his first payoff."

"You two certainly worked fast to solve this mystery," Jill said admiringly.

"And now we can settle back and relax," Frank said with a grin, sinking deeper into his leather chair.

END

78

When the Hardys regained consciousness, they found themselves securely bound in the hold of the yacht.

"Frank, we're moving," Joe said with alarm as he felt the boat rise and fall.

"That was some idea of yours," Frank groaned. "We got the surprise attack."

"How was I to know about the two extra guys down there?" his brother complained.

"We're in real trouble now," Frank went on. "Who knows where this boat is taking us?"

"Well, it's still light out," Joe murmured, glancing out a porthole. "We couldn't have been sailing for too long."

"I can see the headlines now," Frank muttered grimly. "'Hardy Brothers' Bodies Washed Up On California Beach.'"

"Hey, Frank, we may get out of here yet!" Joe suddenly exclaimed. "Listen to that horn."

Wide grins broke out over both detectives' faces.

"The Coast Guard!" Frank said with relief.

Turn to page 108.

79

A moment later, Frank grabbed the man from behind and wrestled the knife from his hand. The two struggled on the deck until the older Hardy finally overpowered the criminal. Then Frank grabbed some rope and securely bound his captive's arms.

"Joe! Where are you?" he yelled when he was finished, and searched the choppy gray water. However, his brother was nowhere in sight!

"Joe!" Frank shouted again. "Joe!"

"Here," an exhausted voice gasped from the side of the boat. Frank ran over and saw ten fingers clinging to the edge. Below them, Joe's bruised but grinning face looked up at him.

Turn to page 114.

80

"Is the name Craig Barlow familiar to you?" Joe asked.

"Barlow?" Eric Barnes responded with surprise. "Of course. Craig's one of our top research engineers."

"We found this chip in the home of Lila Lewis, Barlow's aunt," Frank explained.

"I'll get him in here right now!" the angry executive announced. "He'd better have a mighty good explanation for this."

But when Barnes called the research section of the company, he learned that Craig Barlow had been absent for two days.

"We can't wait for your father to come to Santa Clara," Mr. Barnes said. "You two have got to help me get to the bottom of this mystery. Barlow must be found and questioned! Now!"

"We could interview the people he works with and search his office," Joe suggested.

"Or we could go back to Los Angeles and attempt to locate him there," Frank added.

If you think the Hardys should investigate the Tri-Tech headquarters, turn to page 8.
If you think they should try to locate Craig Barlow in Los Angeles, turn to page 17.

"I'll check out the studio first," the girl detective murmured. She was eager to look for clues in Jack Turner's office.

She walked through the entrance. No one was at the receptionist's desk, so Nancy proceeded toward a row of editing rooms. She heard the soft whir of a movie projector behind the first door. Suddenly it stopped and a man spoke up.

"That wraps it up," he said. "This print will be worth hundreds of thousands on the black market."

"And you're being paid plenty for it, Turner," a second man said.

"I want the rest of the money tonight!" Turner demanded. "If I was caught pirating this film, I'd never get another job in the movie industry."

"Okay, okay. I'll drop it off at your grandmother's place later. Right now I want to get this print out of here."

"I'll meet you at the house in an hour," Turner said.

As the two men came out to the hallway, Nancy quickly slipped into the next room.

Turn to page 82.

82

To her relief, it was empty. Some light filtered in from the outside floodlamps, and she spied a telephone. She dialed *O* for the studio operator and softly asked for the security office. Todd Hanson answered.

"Todd, this is Nancy Drew," she whispered. "I'm in Studio B, where I just overheard Jack Turner making a deal to pirate a film print."

"Has he taken the print out of here yet?" the detective asked.

"His accomplice is leaving with it now," Nancy replied. "I could try to follow him . . . or I could meet you at Lila Lewis's house in an hour. Turner is supposed to get his second payoff then."

If you think Nancy should try to follow the man with the print, turn to page 56.
If you think she should meet the detective at the Lewis mansion in an hour, turn to page 90.

After Nancy returned to the Blakes' house, she explained the mystery of the missing money to Jill.

"Poor Jack!" the dark-haired girl exclaimed. "I hope he's learned his lesson."

83

"I think he has," the young sleuth replied. "Now I'm going to call Frank and Joe at the Silicon Valley computer firm. When I asked Jack about that chip we found, he explained that he had lost it. It belongs to one of the editing machines in his studio."

"Ask Frank and Joe to come back to the house," Jill called after her friend. "I'll give you all a well-deserved tour of Los Angeles tomorrow!"

END

84

Later that day, when Frank and Joe arrived at the Lewis mansion, they saw Nancy and Jill standing on the front steps with a young man.

"What happened?" the titian-blonde sleuth exclaimed as she ran up to them.

"Peter was guilty, all right," Frank replied. "He was part of a ring that was smuggling illegal aliens into the States. The money Jill saw last night was his payoff for providing rich people with inexpensive—and unlawful—help. We caught him with his accomplice by the docks."

"They're both in the custody of the police now," Joe went on. "Peter's friend got away in his boat, but the Coast Guard apprehended him later."

Turn to page 85.

From page 84

"Great!" Nancy said, then led the Hardys back to Jill and the young man, who had long, curly hair.

"Frank, Joe, I'd like you to meet Jack Turner," she said.

"I came to my grandmother's house today to look for a computer chip I'd lost last night," Jack explained. "Nancy told me all about the mystery I got involved with while checking out the place for possible trouble. Trouble was all around me, and I never even noticed!"

"Wait until Miss Lewis returns from Europe and hears this story," Jill exclaimed.

"One thing is for sure," Frank added with a wink. "She'll have to find a new gardener."

END

86

The following day, Nancy sat with the Hardys and Jill on the Blakes' patio. Frank and Joe had just returned to Los Angeles, having learned that the computer chip was worthless.

"Jack Turner was very surprised to find the police waiting for him instead of his payoff," Nancy told the group. "He's in custody now."

"Good work, Nancy," Joe said with admiration.

"That pirated print would have been sold on the black market for videocassettes," the girl detective explained. "I can see why the movie studio was relieved to get it back."

"What film was it?" Jill asked curiously.

Nancy laughed. "You won't believe it, but it was called *The Big Payoff!*"

END

Joe dodged through the groups of people milling about in the terminal. He nervously looked at his watch. There were only ten minutes until takeoff! In the corridor leading to the gate, he saw a line of passengers waiting to pass through the security check.

"Wow!" the detective murmured to himself. "There he is!"

Craig Barlow was just about to go through the detection frame and put a large briefcase on the conveyor belt that ran past an X ray device.

I can't afford to wait in this line, Joe decided. *I'll never catch him if I do.*

Making apologies, he moved right behind Barlow. He noticed a door marked *Office* several yards to the left in the corridor ahead. Quickly, Joe formulated a daring plan. He cut in front of Barlow, who was waiting for his briefcase to come back into sight on the other end of the conveyor belt. When it appeared, the young detective grabbed it and sped away.

"Hey! That's my briefcase!" he heard Barlow's angry voice protest behind him. But before the suspect could catch him, Joe darted into the security office and laid the briefcase on the counter in front of a security official.

Turn to page 89.

"That punk just stole my case," Barlow cried, rushing into the office. "I have a flight to catch, and I want it back immediately!"

"My name is Joe Hardy," the amateur detective said to the bewildered officer. "I'm working for a computer firm, and I have good reason to believe that this briefcase contains stolen hardware. Please call Eric Barnes at Tri-Tech Industries to confirm my story."

A look of panic flashed over Craig Barlow's handsome face. He hesitated for a second, then dashed from the room.

"Stop that man!" the officer called out into the hallway.

Barlow was quickly apprehended by two guards at the security check. Frank arrived just as the suspect was brought back into the office.

Turn to page 103.

90

"We'd better drive to the Lewis house right away and set up surveillance," Todd Hanson said. "We'll catch both these crooks red-handed."

"I'll meet you at the main gate," Nancy agreed. "I'm driving a green Porsche."

"Be careful that you're not seen by Turner," the detective warned.

"I will," Nancy promised and hung up the telephone. Cautiously, she crept out of Studio B, cast a quick glance into the parking lot, and saw both Jack Turner and his accomplice driving away. She got into her car and proceeded to the gate. A short time later, Todd Hanson and two security men joined her.

"The Los Angeles police are sending two men in a cruiser to Lila Lewis's place," Hanson explained. "We'd better hurry to meet them there."

Half an hour later, Nancy ran into the Blake house to explain the situation to Jill. The young girl looked shocked when she learned that Jack Turner was guilty of a crime.

"Lila will be devastated when she finds out," Jill said.

Nancy nodded sadly. "Well, I'm going over there now. You stay here; I'll be back shortly."

Turn to page 101.

"This is blackmail, Jack!" Miss Quinn protested. "I trusted you once with my secret . . . and now . . . now . . ." The actress broke off and started to cry.

"I trusted you, too," Turner said heartlessly. "And you betrayed me by going out with that rich producer. If you don't come up with the cash, I'll call a Hollywood gossip columnist."

"All right, I'll get the money somehow," the starlet promised. "My career would be ruined if you told the press what you know."

Nancy didn't wait to hear more. She bravely walked into view. "I just overheard your conversation," she announced to the startled couple. "And I know all about the briefcase full of money you had at your grandmother's house last night, Mr. Turner."

"Who are you?" the young man demanded.

"My name is Nancy Drew," the girl answered. "I'm an amateur detective, and I intend to help Miss Quinn get her money back."

"Did you hire her?" Jack Turner angrily asked the actress.

"No, I didn't, but I'm glad you're here, Miss Drew," the starlet replied.

Turn to page 92.

92

"I know who your grandmother is, Mr. Turner," Nancy went on. "And I'm sure she would be very interested in your career as a blackmailer."

"You can't tell her about this," the young man cried. "She'd cut me out of her will!"

"Then the solution is simple," the pretty sleuth went on. "You return Miss Quinn's money and never bother her again. In exchange, I'll keep your secret."

Turner's face was flushed an angry red, but he nodded in agreement.

"I'll bring back the cash tonight," he muttered to the actress. Then he turned quickly and walked to his car.

"Miss Drew, how can I ever thank you!" Jennifer Quinn exclaimed. "This has been a nightmare for me."

"I'm glad I could help," Nancy replied. "There is one thing, though . . . ," she added with a twinkle in her blue eyes. "Could you autograph one of your pictures: 'To Frank and Joe Hardy'?"

Turn to page 100.

Nancy stayed frozen in place, staring at the knife in the man's hand. She saw the frightened look on Jill's face and became worried that the girl might do something rash and get hurt.

"You're right," she said calmly to the intruder. "We shouldn't have looked through Peter's personal belongings. We'll leave now and forget about the whole thing."

"Not so fast!" he snarled, jabbing the knife toward them.

Just as Jill let out a scream of panic, Nancy heard the door of the cottage open. Seconds later, Frank and Joe rushed in. The older Hardy knocked the knife out of the intruder's hand with a strong karate chop. Then he tackled the man and threw him to the ground.

"I'll call the police," Joe exclaimed. "It looks like we came back just in time!"

Turn to page 107.

94

The pretty sleuth decided to pursue the man who had vanished into the dark streets of the old-European set.

I hope I remember my way around here, she thought as she followed him, trying to recall the studio tour she had taken that afternoon. Suddenly, she heard the murmur of voices from the other side of a make-believe house. She pressed her body against its wall and crept silently forward. As she rounded the corner of the house, she saw the man's face in the moonlight and recognized him as Jack Turner from the photograph she had seen. He was speaking with another man, who had a mustache and wore an expensive suit.

Just then, Nancy caught her foot on an electric cord that had been left by the film crew. She fell forward, her body making a dull thud on the cobble-stoned street.

"Let's get out of here!" she heard one of the men whisper.

Turn to page 95.

From page 94

As Nancy picked herself up, she saw the men hurrying through the movie lot. She followed as quickly as possible, but lost sight of them as she rounded the clock tower at the end of the European street. Ahead of her were two more movie sets. One was a haunted house sitting on a hill. The other was a medieval castle towering above the lot.

"They must have gone into one of those places!" the girl detective murmured with frustration. "But which one?"

If you think Nancy should go into the haunted house,
turn to page 98.
If you think she should enter the medieval castle, turn to
page 110.

From page 76

96

"So Barlow confessed," Nancy said after she heard the Hardys' story later that night. The three young detectives and Jill Blake had met for a celebration dinner at a Mexican restaurant near the airport.

"That's right," Joe confirmed. "He was in such a panic about going to jail that he told the whole story. A computer company in Japan was paying him to steal secrets from Tri-Tech. Two days ago, a contact dropped off a payment for him at Lila Lewis's mansion. Today, he was flying off to Tokyo to deliver samples of computer hardware."

"He would have gotten away with it, too, if Jill hadn't seen the briefcase full of money," Frank added.

"The credit really goes to you," Jill said, looking at the Hardys with admiring eyes.

"Jill's right," Nancy agreed with a smile. "You two are really high-tech detectives!"

END

Late that night, Frank and Joe sat with Eric Barnes in his office at Tri-Tech industries. The Hardys had brought back Barlow's briefcase rull of top-secret printouts.

"Barlow was selling your research secrets to an up-start computer company for a million dollars!" Joe said, shaking his head in amazement. "The man who came to meet him at the yacht club was the president of the company."

"Craig Barlow spilled out the whole story after we called the police," Frank explained. "He had used Lila Lewis's mansion as a drop-off point for his first payment. When Jill walked in on him, he got scared and changed his next meeting to the Pacifica Yacht Club."

"Thanks to you, our problem with leaks should be over," Eric Barnes said. "When your father gets into town, I'll have to tell him this case is already solved!"

END

98

Nancy stared at the dilapidated haunted house outlined in the moonlight against the evening sky. Then she walked up its crumbling stone steps. A door creaked in the dark structure, sending shivers down her spine.

"They must be in there," she whispered to herself as she reached the entrance. With great care, she pushed open the wooden door and slipped inside.

The girl detective found herself standing in a huge paneled room. Even in the dim light, she could see silvery cobwebs drooping from the ceiling. Suddenly, there was a thump above her head. Apparently, someone was upstairs.

Nancy crept toward the staircase. Cautiously, she tiptoed up, fearful that the creaking steps would give her away. At last, she reached the top and moved silently to an open door.

"I want you to delay the shooting for at least a week!" a man demanded. "My company wants its film to be released before this one is even printed!"

Nancy peered inside the room and saw Jack Turner pacing the floor.

Turn to page 99.

"I'll do what I can!" he promised. "Today I tried to sabotage the lighting system, but the engineers fixed it right away."

"We've paid you a lot of money, Turner!" the other man threatened. "And we expect results!"

Just then, Jack Turner glanced nervously toward the door. Nancy jerked her head back, but she was too late. He had seen her!

"Someone's snooping on us!" he hissed to his companion, and rushed toward her.

The young sleuth ran down the hallway. At the end was a door that stood slightly ajar. Nancy quickly ran through it. Suddenly, she screamed. The floor had given way beneath her, and she was falling into blackness!

Turn to page 105.

From page 92

100

The following day, Nancy proudly handed over the autographed photo to the boys when they returned to the Blake mansion.

"You met Jennifer Quinn!" Joe exclaimed, staring with admiration at the lovely actress's picture.

"And all we did was chase down a false lead at Silicon Valley," Frank added with exasperation.

"I solved the mystery of the missing money, too," the girl detective announced. "But that's a secret between Miss Quinn and me."

"I still can't believe it," Joe said, shaking his head in mock tragedy. "If we had followed Nancy's lead, *we'd* share a secret with Jennifer Quinn!"

END

When Jack Turner let himself into his grandmother's house, Nancy, Todd, and two police officers were hiding in the darkened living room. Jack nervously paced the floor until he heard a knock on the door leading to the garden. As soon as he had let his accomplice in, the lights flashed on.

"Stay right where you are!" the gruff voice of a policeman ordered the startled thieves.

"What are you doing in my grandmother's house?" Turner demanded weakly.

Todd Hanson stepped forward and took a heavy briefcase from the mustached accomplice. He set it on a table and opened it. Inside were hundreds of neatly stacked bills!

"You're under arrest," the studio detective declared.

"Take us to where you put that pirated film!" the policeman ordered the accomplice. "Then we're going to headquarters to hear your stories."

As the officers led away the criminals, Todd Hanson looked at Nancy with admiration.

"You've done it again," he said. "I wish you were in Los Angeles to stay. We could use your help more often."

Turn to page 102.

102

Nancy laughed. "I'll only be here two more days," she said. "And I'd like to spend them the way I had planned—as a vacation!"

END

The officer snapped open the briefcase, and Joe let out a low whistle.

"Look, it's full of chips just like the one we found at the Lewis mansion!" he exclaimed.

"I'm afraid you'll be missing your flight," the officer informed Barlow. "There are several telephone calls I need to make about you."

"How do you know so much?" the angry young man snapped at the Hardys.

"You made a mistake when you were at your aunt's house two nights ago," Frank replied. "You lost a chip when you went to pick up that very same briefcase, which was full of thousands of dollars!"

Turn to page 112.

Her fall was finally broken by an air mattress. She blinked her eyes, trying to focus on where she was. She felt narrow walls around her and realized she was trapped.

A moment later, she heard scuffling above her and the sound of indistinct voices. Then a light shone through the door. It had been open all along.

"Nancy, are you all right?" Todd Hanson called down.

"Yes, I am," she replied. "Did you catch Turner?"

"Red-handed, thanks to you," the studio detective said. "Now let's get you out of here!"

Within a few minutes, he lowered a rope ladder. She quickly scrambled up and once again found herself in the hallway of the haunted house.

"I saw you come back to the studio," the detective explained. "You led me and my men right to these crooks!"

"Turner was being paid to sabotage one of your films!" Nancy announced, watching as four security guards led the handcuffed criminals away.

"We checked his briefcase and found two thousand dollars in small bills," Todd Hanson added. "But you've saved the studio a lot more money than that!"

Turn to page 106.

106

"I also got my first chance to be a stuntwoman." The pretty sleuth chuckled, shaking her reddish-blonde hair. "I think I'll stick with being a detective!"

END

When the gardener returned to his cottage an hour later, he was immediately handcuffed by two waiting police officers. The young detectives listened as he confessed that he had been stealing valuables from the homes of Miss Lewis's neighbors. His curly-haired accomplice had already admitted to being the fence for the stolen goods, and to having dropped off Peter's payment at the mansion the night before.

When the police took the two thieves away, Nancy let out a sigh of relief.

"That solves the mystery of the missing money," she said. "Peter managed to get away with the briefcase while Jill was out of the house."

"And Jack Turner turned out to be a false lead," Joe added. "It looks like he's not the only one around here with long, curly hair."

"We can forget this computer chip, too," Frank said, tossing it in the air. "But I will double-check it with Dad."

"Now let's get back to the house," Nancy suggested. "I'm ready for a real vacation."

END

From page 78

108

They listened intently as a Coast Guard cutter pulled up beside the yacht. There was the scuffling sound of men coming aboard. Then, suddenly, the hatch opened, and a face peered down at them.

"Dad!" Frank and Joe exclaimed in a surprised chorus.

"You boys are lucky I check up on you once in a while," Fenton Hardy said with a relieved smile.

"But you're not supposed to be here yet," Joe pointed out.

"Thank goodness, I came to Santa Clara ahead of time," his father replied. "When I called Eric Barnes at Tri-Tech, he explained the mystery you were tracking down. I drove straight to the yacht club to find you. An old sailor there had seen you disappear down the hatch of this boat. So I called the Coast Guard immediately."

"What about Barlow?" Frank asked as Mr. Hardy untied them.

"He's been taken into custody," his father answered. "And so has his partner in the scheme, the head of a foreign computer firm. Barlow was being paid to steal Tri-Tech's development secrets."

Turn to page 109.

The two brothers and Fenton Hardy climbed up the stairs onto the deck. They watched as the Coast Guard took the suspects and their accomplices onto the cutter.

"I told the captain that you two could bring this yacht back into port," Mr. Hardy announced. "Is that all right with you?"

"Is it ever!" Joe exclaimed.

"Set sail for California!" Frank added with a grin.

END

Nancy hesitated a second and then followed the path that led to the huge stone fortress. As she walked across the wooden drawbridge into the castle, she heard the fall of footsteps inside.

Quickly, the young sleuth hurried toward a large banquet hall in the middle of the structure. The dim lighting concealed her as she slipped behind a suit of armor on one side of the room. Jack Turner and the mustached man she had seen previously were standing by a wooden trestle table only yards away.

"Here's your second payoff," the man said to Turner. "I don't want this film to see the light of day. That director had no right to fire me. And I'm going to get my revenge!"

"Don't worry, Lou," Jack assured him. "I'll make sure this film is destroyed in the editing room. But it's going to cost you another five grand."

Lou flipped open a case he was carrying and revealed its contents. Nancy peeked out from behind the suit of armor and saw hundreds of dollars. Jack Turner greedily stuffed them into his briefcase.

"I'm warning you," Lou said, "you'll only get more money after the film is destroyed!"

Turn to page 111.

Just then, Nancy accidentally brushed against a sword that was attached to the armored knight's side. It fell to the floor with a loud clatter, and the girl fled instantly.

The two men whirled around and saw her escaping from the room. Turner grabbed his money, and the crooks rushed after her.

Nancy saw a flight of stairs several feet away leading into the basement. She darted toward them and descended into the cellar of the castle.

The men scrambled down the stairs after her.

Turn to page 115.

112

After Barlow had been taken into custody, Joe and Frank returned to the Blake house, where they found Jill and Nancy waiting for them.

"No wonder my investigation of Jack Turner was a dead end!" Nancy declared after she heard their story. "I was following the wrong curly-haired man!"

"Eric Barnes is driving to L.A. right now to press charges," Frank explained. "But Barlow refused to admit anything. He just called his lawyer."

"The police suspect he is involved in high-tech espionage," Joe went on. "The money Jill saw must have been one of his payoffs. He was probably flying to Hong Kong to deliver those top-secret computer parts."

"Wait until Dad hears about this!" Frank added with a grin. "We solved his case before he even started it!"

END

"We've been having real trouble here at Tri-Tech," he remarked. "Our product development is one of the best in Silicon Valley. But we've been plagued by leaks and by thefts of parts. It's a bad situation!"

Frank reached into his pocket and pulled out the chip he had found on the floor of the Lewis mansion.

"Can you identify this, Mr. Barnes?" he requested.

The vice-president took the object and carefully inspected it. The boys watched as he clenched his jaw in anger.

"Where did you find this?" he demanded.

"In a mansion in the hills above Los Angeles," Joe explained. "We were investigating the disappearance of a briefcase full of money. So far, we haven't been able to put the pieces of the puzzle together."

"This chip is a piece of a very valuable puzzle," Eric Barnes declared. "It's part of our new PC—personal computer—the one we plan to market next year. The mystery is . . . how did it get out of here?"

Turn to page 80.

114

Late that afternoon, Joe sat on the Blakes' terrace, holding an ice pack against his swollen cheek.

"Poor Joe," Jill said sympathetically, "do you still want to go surfing tomorrow?"

"I sure do!" the blond detective replied. "We've got those criminals locked up in jail, and I'm ready for some fun!"

"The police were waiting for the gardener when he came to clear his things out," Nancy explained. "He confessed his part in a smuggling ring that was bringing illegal aliens into the States."

"The money you saw last night, Jill, was the cash that prospective employers had given Peter to deliver illegal help to them. Aliens work for much lower wages than anyone else, so Peter and his friend were valuable to greedy employers."

"I'm relieved that Jack Turner is innocent," Jill said. "He stopped by this afternoon just after you drove off. He told me he had come to check on his grandmother's house last night. He accidentally scared off the gardener, who was counting his payoff in Miss Lewis's living room."

"Peter's aunt was visiting him at the cottage," Nancy added, "and he didn't want her to see the money, so he had it delivered to the mansion."

Turn to page 73.

At the bottom, was a dark room leading to a stone-walled dungeon. The sleuth noticed that its spiked iron bars were raised up to the top.

Thank goodness I took that studio tour, she thought, and hid behind a stone column outside the cell.

"Where is she!" Jack Turner hissed with frustration as he reached the dungeon.

Nancy took a ring from her finger and tossed it into the cell, hitting its stone wall.

"In there!" Lou exclaimed, running with Turner into the dark enclosure.

As soon as both men were inside, Nancy pressed a button the tour guide had shown her. With a loud clang, the spiked gate of the dungeon crashed down to the floor!

The young detective walked out from her hiding place and smiled at the two prisoners.

Turn to page 116.

116

"I'll be right back with the police, Mr. Turner," she said wryly to the young man. "And I'm afraid you're in for an unhappy ending!"

Turn to page 31.

Frank drove at the maximum speed limit through the busy Los Angeles traffic to the international airport.

117

"We want Terminal B," Joe said with nervous anticipation as he read the airline signs on the service road.

Frank swung the car into a parking place near the terminal, then the sleuths ran into the building.

"There are two flights leaving in the next fifteen minutes!" Joe said breathlessly after he read the computerized board showing arrivals and departures.

"We don't know which one Barlow is on, and passenger information is confidential."

"We'll have to split up, then," Frank announced. "You go to Gate Twenty for the plane to Hong Kong. I'll check out Gate Thirty-two for the flight to Tokyo."

If you want to follow Joe, turn to page 87.
If you want to follow Frank, turn to page 61.